For E

Happy ...

love,
Auntie Rena
(mimi's sister ☺)

# I Just See YOU!

by Lyn Wells Clark

Illustrations by Lorena Mary Hart

**Blue-Eyed Star Creations**

I Just See You
by Lyn Wells Clark
Illustrations by Lorena Mary Hart
Published by Blue-Eyed Star Creations, LLC and Carolyn Clark
2 Old Forest St., Middleton, MA 01949
blue-eyedstarcreations.com
© 2022 Blue-Eyed Star Creations, LLC and Carolyn Clark
All rights reserved. No portion of this book may be reproduced
in any form without permission from the publisher,
except as permitted by U.S. copyright law.
For permissions contact: help@blue-eyedstarcreations.com
ISBN: 978-0-9994409-7-1

This book is dedicated to my amazing and kind-hearted son Justin, who has always accepted people for who they are. So proud of the wonderful man you've become.

Love you, Bud!

All my love and gratitude
to my wonderful husband
and children.

"Hey little loris,
 what do you see,
 what do you see when you see me?"

"Do you see my big hairy shape?" asked the big and hairy ape.

"You are big and hairy, it is true, but my furry friend, I just see YOU!"

"Do you see my boney joints?"
the porcupine asked with pointy points.

You have boney joints and pointy points too, but my old friend, I just see YOU!"

"Do you see a wise, clever fowl?" asked the wise and clever owl.

"You are wise and clever,
it is true,
but my smart friend,
I just see YOU!"

"Do you see a long, lanky giraffe?"
the lanky giraffe asked with a laugh.

"You are long and lanky too,
 but my funny friend, I just see YOU!"

"Do you see a slick, slimy frog?"
asked the slimy frog sitting on a log.

"You are slick and slimy, it is true,
but my slippery friend, I just see YOU!"

"Well my friends,
what do you see,
what do you see when you see me?"
asked the loris timidly.

"I am quite small.
I have big eyes.
I am not fast.
I am not wise."

"While all of those things may be true, our dear little friend, we just see...

## ABOUT THE AUTHOR

Lyn Wells Clark resides in Middleton, Massachusetts, where she and her husband, Michael, raised their children. *I Just See You!* follows Lyn's books *The Unlikely Adventure of a Turtle, a Mouse and a Shark*, *Sleep Well My Baby*, *The Monster Who Had a Kind Face*, and *The Girl Who Loved Yellow*. All five books are beautifully written and illustrated. It is always important to Lyn that her books be joyful and whimsical so that even small children unable to read will be drawn to them.

CPSIA information can be obtained
at www.ICGtesting.com
Printed in the USA
BVHW062102271022
650492BV00002B/2